# Virtual Friend

## by

## Mary Hoffman

## Illustrated by Shaun McLaren

You do not need to read this page - just get on with the book!

First published 1998 in Great Britain by
Barrington Stoke Ltd
10 Belford Terrace, Edinburgh, EH4 3DQ
Reprinted 1998, 1999, 2000

This edition first published 2001
Reprinted 2001

ISBN 1-902260-85-6
Previously published by Barrington Stoke Ltd under ISBN 1-902260-00-7

Printed by Polestar AUP Aberdeen Ltd

## Meet The Author - MARY HOFFMAN

*What is your favourite animal?*
Any kind of cat
*What is your favourite boy's name?*
Lorenzo
*What is your favourite girl's name?*
Arianwen
*What is your favourite food?*
Indian
*What is your favourite music?*
Opera - especially Wagner and Mozart
*What is your favourite hobby?*
Reading and swimming - but not at the same time!

## Meet The Illustrator - SHAUN MCLAREN

*What is your favourite animal?*
A gnu
*What is your favourite boy's name?*
Joe
*What is your favourite girl's name?*
Joyce (my wife)
*What is your favourite food?*
Peanut butter and banana sandwiches
*What is your favourite music?*
A bit of everything!
*What is your favourite hobby?*
Balancing things on the end of my pencil

For Ben Fairbank,
who liked the idea

# Contents

# Chapter One

Ben Silver was bored. He was bored because he had nothing to do. And he had nothing to do because he had no one to do anything with. He had no friends. Not because there was anything wrong with Ben. It just wasn't fair.

The only reason he had no friends was that his father had moved with him to a new town when he got a new job. And a new town meant a new school. And it wasn't even a new term. School had been back for three weeks and Ben had missed the scrimmage of the first few days.

That's when everyone finds classrooms, loos, their own special bit of playground and their own special group of people like them.

So Ben was lonely at school. And at the weekends he was lonely at home too. He was an only child.

'Just as well,' Dad often said, sighing, his eyes filling with tears. Ben's Dad was quite soppy. But he had a reason to be. Ben's Mum had died two years ago and he and Dad had both been a bit likely to burst into tears for a long time. But Ben was getting over it better than Dad.

He was a good Dad, no doubt about that. Only he worked so hard to make a good life for both of them that he had to go where the work was. He often had to work on Saturdays and Sundays. And that left Ben with nothing to do and no one to do it with.

Computers. That was Dad's line. But Ben wasn't interested in computers, except for playing games, which was only allowed when Dad wasn't using his for work.

'What are you going to do today?' asked Dad that Saturday morning. Ben wondered whether to make up lots of exciting invitations. But he realised that his Dad probably wouldn't know he was joking. So he just shrugged.

'Only I've got to work till lunchtime, but I thought this afternoon we might pop in and see Vince.'

Ben goggled. Dad had a friend?

'You know, Vince next door. The one with the shed.'

Ben realised too late that he should have made something up that he had to do urgently. Dad's friend was the nutter next door, Vince

Riggs. Other people had ordinary garden sheds, the kind you put spades and lawnmowers in. Vince had a shed the size of a second house, taking up all the space where other people might have a lawn or a pond with fishing gnomes.

'The mad professor?' Ben said slowly, still trying to think of a way out.

'Yes,' said Dad. 'He's very interesting actually. I had a long chat with him over the fence yesterday afternoon when I was hanging out the washing. You'll never guess what he's got in that shed of his.'

'A monster with a bolt through its neck?' suggested Ben. 'A home-made space rocket that runs on lemonade?'

Dad tapped the side of his nose.

'Close,' he said. 'All will be revealed after lunch. Now why don't you go and get the

shopping, if you've got nothing else on and I can deal with the bugs in this computer program.'

It was no good protesting when Dad talked about his work like that. Ben picked up the list and some money from the hall table.

Coming out of the supermarket an hour later, he saw some boys from school. They were rollerblading down the High Street, slaloming round old ladies with shopping bags, listening to loud walkmans, drinking coke out of cans and generally looking as if they were having fun.

'Tsk, tsk, tsk,' muttered a large woman with a shopping trolley piled high with dog food. 'Young people today!'

She glared at Ben. Then she noticed that he was meekly carrying a shopping bag full of groceries and a neat shopping list. She changed her frown to a horrible leer. Ben supposed it was meant to be a smile.

'Good boy,' she said and gave him a chocolate bar.

The whooping, skating, happy boys whooshed past just at that moment. Ben had the awful idea that they might think the dog food lady was his mother. He thanked her politely for the chocolate and ran home.

*****

Vince Riggs was delighted to see them both. His house was the tidiest and cleanest Ben had ever seen, but Vince took them straight through it to the back garden.

'The missus has gone bowling,' said Vince, as if that explained everything. 'So we've got the place to ourselves.'

He led them out to the massive shed and Ben noticed it had a satellite dish on the top. He also noticed a huge sign over the door which he hadn't seen before.

'MR V.R.' it said, inside a huge pair of goggles.

Ben stared at the notice.

'Mister Vee Arr. Get it? Vince Riggs - Virtual Reality!' said Vince.

Dad beamed at Ben. This was the surprise. More computers. Vince was not just a nutter. He was a nutter with a house-proud wife who made him do his hobby in a huge garden shed. And his hobby was putting on a helmet and gloves and playing at being somewhere else. Ben's heart sank.

And then Vince opened the shed door.

'Wow!' said Ben.

He had never seen anything like it in his life.

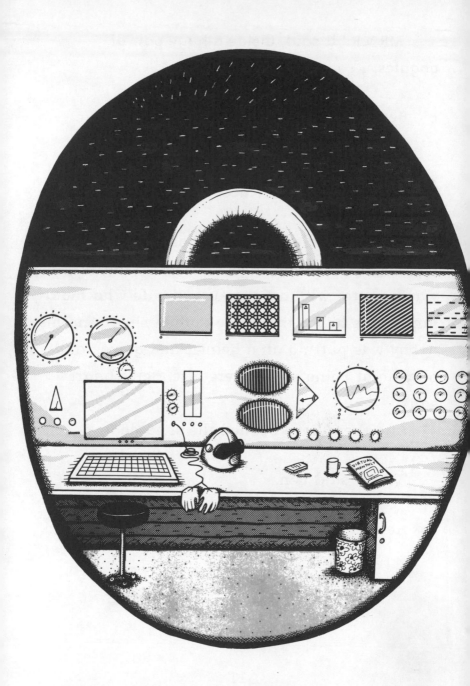

# Chapter Two

'Impressed, huh?' said Vince.

Ben nodded, speechless. The shed was filled with banks of screens and consoles and all the latest equipment. It looked like the bridge of the Starship Enterprise. If this was a hobby, Vince sure had a lot of pocket money.

'Vince is setting up his own business,' said Dad.

'Yup,' said Vince happily throwing a few switches and pressing buttons. 'It'll be Mister V.R. *plc* by the end of the year. Course I'll have to get proper offices by then. Sylvia says she's not having this lot taking up space in the garden any longer than she can help. Wants a lawn.'

Vince looked at Ben and Dad as if to say, 'Who can understand women? Why would they possibly want a boring square of grass when they could have a shed full of Virtual Reality?'

'I mean, she could come here and see lawns like at Wimbledon any day of the week,' said Vince. 'And I wouldn't have to mow them. But she wants the real thing.'

'Can I have a go?' Ben asked.

These were the words Vince loved to hear and he had soon given Ben and Dad some very impressive headsets, like biker helmets with built-in goggles. He also gave them gloves that had pads on every fingertip.

'Cybergloves,' explained Vince. 'State
of the art. You'll be able to touch and feel
everything you see.'

Vince had an enormous number of programs
to choose from. While Dad was dithering
between snowboarding in the Rockies and a
safari in Kenya, Vince pushed one towards Ben.
It was called 'Virtual Friend'.

'Here, Ben, have a go at this one. It's like
Tamagotchi, only you can invent a human pal
for yourself.'

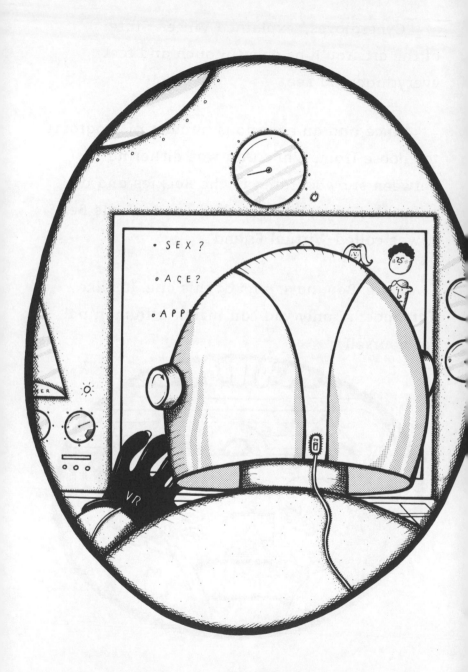

Ben was not sure. Had Dad been telling Vince about him? But he couldn't help being interested. A friend you could invent for yourself sounded good. He lowered the goggles over his eyes and Vince helped him with the controls.

SEX -      male

AGE -      12

APPEARANCE ...

Ben chose a black boy from the range of faces that flashed up before his eyes on the screen. He invented a tall, thin boy with dreadlocks and a wicked grin. The sort of boy you could hang out with and have silly jokes with. Ben quickly programmed in a good sense of humour. By the time he had made all his choices and filled in all his options, he had put in everything he wanted in a friend at his new school.

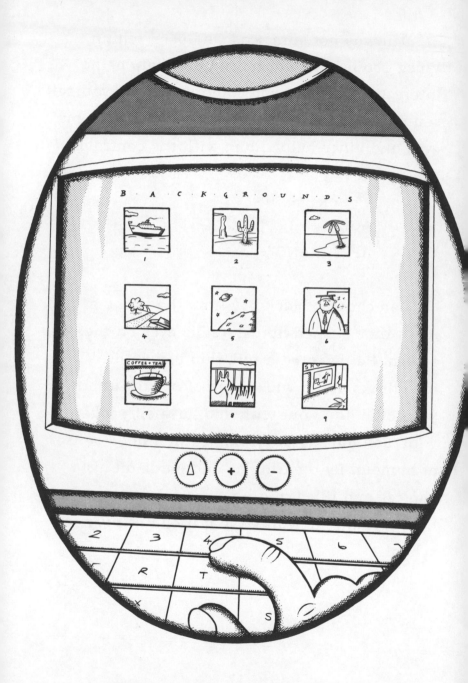

'Now all you've got to do is to give him a name,' said Vince, 'And you're ready to go.'

Ben thought.

'Rory,' he said. That sounded sort of loud and confident. 'Rory Polestar.'

'Sounds like a pop singer,' said Vince, his fingers flying over the control pad. 'Now, choose a background setting and you can go off and play with your mate.'

'Wow!' yelled Dad from the other side of the shed.

He was jerking his body around most strangely. It looked as if he'd gone for the snowboarding.

Ben chose PARK from a menu that had SCHOOL, ZOO, MALL, COFFEE SHOP and some others, and pulled on the gloves.

The shed disappeared and Ben was standing on a long, gravel drive. There were trees and grass on both sides. In the distance was a pond with toy sailboats on it. Dogs raced across the grass barking and Ben could hear birds chirping and the bell of an ice-cream van.

'Awesome!' he breathed.

Ben heard a crunching, growling sound behind him, coming closer. He turned around and there was ... Rory Polestar! He was just as Ben had imagined him, big grin, dreadlocks and all. He was on a skateboard and he came skimming towards Ben along the path, holding his hand up.

Wham!

Ben felt Rory slap his hand so hard, it almost knocked him off balance. His palm tingled. He really felt it. Rory was as real as Ben's Dad.

'Hey!' said Rory. 'Let's go to the ramp.'

He sped off.

'But I haven't got ...' Ben started to say, then looked down at his feet. There was a skateboard underneath them. 'All right!' said Ben and took off after Rory.

As they swooped and spun and leapt and swerved around the ramp, Ben wondered with a part of his mind how Vince was doing it. This was nothing like the VR game he had once played at the Trocadero.

He could almost smell the flowers in the park beds beyond the ramp. And when Rory suggested they get an ice-cream, he could feel the coolness on his tongue, the scrunch of the cone against his teeth.

For a fleeting second Ben saw himself sticking his tongue out into the empty air in nutty Vince's shed.

'I must look a right wally,' he thought.

But then he forgot everything except being in the park with Rory, his friend. Ben felt as if he had known him for years.

Rory chatted about his large family, his twin sisters, his uncles who were in a Reggae band, his Mum who was big and cuddly, until Ben felt he knew them all too.

'You should come home and have some of her fried chicken,' Rory was saying, when something suddenly went wrong with the program.

Menus flashed up rapidly before Ben's eyes, he saw SCHOOL in big letters, QUIT? and SAVE? but everything happened so quickly he didn't have time to reach his control pad. Rory Polestar seemed to melt, like an ice lolly dropped on the pavement. The park disappeared and Ben was in the dark.

He took off the helmet, but it was still dark. He heard Vince cursing and stumbling about and the sound of dead switches being thrown.

'What is it?' came Dad's voice.

'The power's down,' said Vince.

And then a big shaft of light lit up the shed as the door was flung open. A large woman in a purple tracksuit stood in the doorway and she did not look happy.

'Sylvia,' thought Ben.

'I'll say the power's down, you daft pudding,' said the woman. 'And you know why? Because you didn't pay that monster electricity bill we had for all the power your silly toys use up. And they've cut us off. And I can't even put

the kettle on for a cuppa, let alone make our dinner. You'll have to buy fish and chips.'

'I think we'd better be off, Vince,' said Dad quickly. 'Come on Ben. Thanks for the game.'

# Chapter Three

The rest of the weekend was even duller than usual. The glimpse Ben had had of what it would be like to have a good friend to hang around with had made his real situation even worse.

'I know just how you feel,' said Dad when Ben tried to talk to him about it. 'I was just getting the hang of that snowboarding when the power went down.'

But Dad didn't have any idea how Ben felt. He felt as if the colour had gone out of everything and left the world greyer than before.

Monday morning finally came and Ben reluctantly dragged on his uniform.

He walked to school by the longest route possible but still got there too early. He was scuffing his shoes and looking down at the ground when a familiar voice called from the playground.

'Hey, Bendigo!'

'Rory?' said Ben.

He could not believe it. But there was no mistake. Rory Polestar was standing at the gate as real as the gateposts. Already an interested crowd had gathered round the newcomer. But, oh happy day, Rory had all his attention focused on Ben.

And at that moment Ben didn't care that what was happening was impossible. He had

wished for a friend - invented a friend, even - and here he was. Nothing else mattered.

As the two slapped hands, several boys who had ignored Ben before nodded a greeting to him.

'Didn't know you knew him,' muttered one. Ben recognised him as Dylan, the leader of the rollerbladers.

'Know him?' said Rory, flashing his most star-studded smile. 'Why Ben and I go way back. Rory Polestar and Bendigo Quicksilver are the cool rulers. Right, Ben?'

'Right,' said Ben, rejoicing in his new name, which seemed to make him much more interesting. He felt himself growing taller and more confident in Rory's company. And he couldn't help noticing the admiring looks that some of the girls were sending in their direction.

'We gotta talk man,' said Rory, taking him by the arm. 'Let's split.'

Ben felt that all eyes were on them now as they strolled across the playground.

'What happened to you on Saturday?' asked Rory, as if it were the most ordinary question in the world. 'One minute you were there beside me in the park and the next you'd gone.'

Ben didn't know what to say. Rory was the one who had melted. Rory was the one who wasn't real for goodness sake! And then Ben began to get the funniest feeling that perhaps Rory was the real one after all and he, Ben, was the one who had melted.

Ben shook his head to get rid of this scary idea. But before he could think of an answer that made any kind of sense, the bell rang.

'Lesson time!' grinned Rory.

Ben felt his blood run cold. What were the teachers going to make of Rory? He wasn't going to appear on anyone's register, was he? And who were they going to ask about the new boy? Why, who else but his old friend, good old Ben Silver?

Ben wished he still had his virtual reality control pad. Much as he loved having Rory there, he would have pressed DELETE at that moment.

'Hurry up, Ben Silver. Stop daydreaming,' said Mr Crawford, the class teacher.

Ben blinked and looked round. There was no sign of Rory. Perhaps he had imagined the whole thing? He even put his hand on his forehead to see if it felt hot.

But other people in the classroom were looking round too.

'Where's Polestar?' whispered Dylan. 'Bad luck if he's been put in another class.'

'Yes,' said Ben with relief. 'He's not in our class.'

He didn't see Rory for the rest of the morning. Breaktime was taken up with a piano lesson and it wasn't until lunchtime that Ben felt the need of a friend again.

As he lined up for his chips and pasty, Ben thought about last week when he'd sat and eaten his lunch at a table with other people but felt completely alone.

'I wish Rory was here,' he thought.

A tray nudged into his back and there was Rory saying, 'Hey man, what's good to eat in this place?'

The two boys took their trays to the same table and Ben smiled as Dylan and his crowd asked if they could join them. Ben had no idea how it worked, but if he could make Rory appear

and disappear just by wishing, that was OK
by him. That way he could get all the glory
of having him as a friend without having to
explain him to any teachers.

Ben watched Rory carefully. He was wolfing
down a large slice of pizza and chips and taking
huge slurps of chocolate milkshake. Ben reached
out and stole one of Rory's chips and bit into it.
It tasted perfectly normal. Rory grinned and
reached over and took one of Ben's chips in
return.

If Rory wasn't real, he was certainly able
to eat real food. Ben shook his head. He wasn't
going to understand how it worked but his
virtual reality friend was now as real as any
boy in the school.

He didn't see Rory all afternoon, but he was
waiting for Ben at the school gates at home
time. The two boys fell into step as if they had

walked home together all their lives. It wasn't until Ben reached his own gate that he realised he was going to have to ask Rory in.

Dad was at home working and seemed pleased that Ben had brought a friend home. If he noticed anything unusual about Rory, he didn't say anything. After they'd had a couple of cans of coke and two slices each of chocolate cake, Rory wanted to go out in the garden.

He stared at the huge shed on Vince's side of the fence and went very silent. Soon afterwards Rory said it was time he was getting back.

'See ya tomorrow!' he called and skateboarded off down the road. Ben couldn't imagine where he was going.

Ben mooched back into the garden and saw Vince waving at him.

'Hello, Ben,' he said cheerily. 'Sorry about Saturday. The missus was in a bit of a mood.'

'That's OK,' said Ben. 'How's the VR? Have you got the power back on yet?'

'No,' said Vince. 'I've paid the bill but they said they'd have to wait a few days for the cheque to clear. Should be back up by the weekend though.'

Ben thought of a whole week without electric lights, TV, cups of tea, washing machine and toaster. Sylvia was probably still in a mood. Vince must have read Ben's mind.

'The missus has gone to her sister's,' he said and Ben thought he sounded a bit lonely.

'You can come and spend the evening with us,' said Ben. 'I'm sure Dad won't mind. He'd like the company.'

# Chapter Four

It was the least lonely week of Ben and Dad's life. Every day Ben had Rory to hang round with at school. And every evening, as soon as it got dark, Vince came over to their house. It meant Dad had to stop working at about six. And then he and Vince made the most marvellous dinners.

Vince insisted on bringing all the food - 'Least I can do,' he said.

Ben had forgotten what a good cook Dad could be and, with Vince's help, there were

curries, Chinese food, pasta, kebabs - a whole
world tour of goodies.

Ben was happier at school than he had ever
been. It wasn't just Rory. Ben now knew at least
four other boys who called him by his name and
talked to him in class. Even if what they talked
about was Rory. And there was a girl, Gerry,
who was part of the group too. Ben felt himself
beginning to relax.

And at break times, there was always Rory,
ready to do the craziest things. One day he tied
a giant pink ribbon round Mr Crawford's tiny
car, so it sat in the staff car park looking like a
box of chocolates. And he did the most brilliant
graffiti on the dull back wall of the school.
Things like 'Cool Rulers' were written in swirls
of silver and gold and sparkly colours. Some
of the things Rory did were definitely against
the rules. But they were always interesting.

Everything was going fine until Friday (the thirteenth, of course). At lunchtime, Ben did his usual trick of wishing Rory was there and - he wasn't. Ben took his tray and went to sit with Dylan, Gerry and the others. It was very different from a week ago. Now they smiled and moved up to make room for him. But everyone was looking round for Rory.

He didn't come into lunch until they'd nearly finished eating. He looked as if he'd been in a fight. He came straight over to their table.

'Bendigo,' he said. 'I got trouble.'

The others pretended not to listen, while Ben and Rory went into a huddle in the corner.

'What's up?' asked Ben.

Rory spread his hands.

'I don't feel so good today. Brain's on the blink. And then I was coming to meet you when Mr Mills stopped me.'

'The Head? What for?'

'He says he wants to see me in his office straight after lunch. Says my name isn't on his records.'

Ben felt a chill run through his body from head to toe.

'You gotta help me, Ben,' said Rory. 'I don't think I can answer his questions. I don't know if I belong here or not.'

He reached out to put a hand on Ben's shoulder. And for the first time Ben wasn't sure he could feel Rory's touch.

'Look, don't worry,' he said. 'if you don't feel well, you should go home. Mr Mills won't do anything till next week.'

'Yeah,' said Rory. 'Take me home Ben. Take me back to your place.'

There wasn't really anything else Ben could do. He felt responsible for Rory.

'I know how Frankenstein must have felt when his monster got up off the table,' he thought.

Then he felt ashamed of thinking that. Rory wasn't a monster. But Ben had made him. Just as surely as if he'd put him together from bits of other people.

They slipped out of the playground and set off for Ben's house. Luckily Dad was out. Rory looked terrible. Ben wasn't a hundred per cent sure, but he thought Rory might be fading.

'Can't seem to get my breath,' Rory said, putting his hand on his chest. 'Let's go outside and get some air.'

In the garden, Rory moved listlessly to the fence. He seemed drawn to Vince's garden and the shed where it had all begun.

And then it happened.

There was a sudden blaze of noise, light and colour from Vince's shed.

'The power,' said Ben. 'They must have turned the electricity back on.'

He turned to Rory, but his virtual friend had gone, or rather, was going. Ben saw a streak of coloured sparks stretched out into a long, thin shape beside him. It homed its way to the shed like an Exocet.

Out of the air came the voice of Rory Polestar, thin and far-off.

'Going home. See ya, Ben.'

And there was nothing.

*****

At first Ben was in a state of shock. When Dad came in he found Ben still standing transfixed by the garden fence. He was cold and shivering.

So Ben's confused story about bringing Rory home because he wasn't well was soon translated by Dad into Ben not feeling well himself. He seemed to have forgotten all about Rory, even though he'd seen him after school every day that week.

Dad phoned Mr Mills and explained that he thought Ben might be coming down with flu. Then he wrapped Ben in the fleecy car rug and gave him a hot chocolate and two aspirins.

By supper time, Ben had thawed out but he still felt frozen inside. Dad was making Swiss fondue and Vince had brought round a bottle of white wine.

'We're celebrating!' he said.

'What's the occasion?' asked Dad, his glasses steaming up from the melted cheese.

'The power's back on,' said Ben dully.

Vince looked at him sharply.

'How did you know?'

Ben shrugged.

'He's right,' said Vince. 'Came back just after lunch. So this is our last little get-together, Sylvia's coming back tomorrow. I just wanted to thank you for all you've done for me this week. Couldn't have coped without you.'

Ben stayed wrapped up in the rug, poking his chunk of bread on a mini toasting-fork into the sticky mess of cheese.

'Do you want to come and have another go at the VR, Ben?' asked Vince.

Ben shook his head.

'Not yet,' he said. 'Maybe later.'

Next day, Ben felt almost back to normal.

'What are you doing today?' asked Dad.

But before he could answer, the doorbell rang. It was Dylan, Gerry and two other kids from school.

'Do you want to come skating?' asked Dylan.

'I haven't got any skates,' said Ben.

But Gerry had brought her brother's, so Ben did go with them. He had a great time. He kept expecting them to mention Rory, but they seemed to have forgotten him - just like Dad.

When Ben got back, Dad had lunch on the table.

'Hello, Ben,' he said. 'I'm so glad you're making friends at your new school.'

'Yeah,' said Ben. 'It's all right here.'

And for now it was.

# Who is Barrington Stoke?

Barrington Stoke was a famous and much-loved story-teller. He travelled from village to village carrying a lantern to light his way. He arrived as it grew dark and when the young boys and girls of the village saw the glow of his lantern, they hurried to the central meeting place. They were full of excitement and expectation, for his stories were always wonderful.

Then Barrington Stoke set down his lantern. In the flickering light the listeners were enthralled by his tales of adventure, horror and mystery. He knew exactly what they liked best and he loved telling a good story. And another. And then another. When the lantern burned low and dawn was nearly breaking, he slipped away. He was gone by morning, only to appear the next day in some other village to tell the next story.

If you loved this story,
find out what happens next in..

# Virtual Friends Again

## by Mary Hoffman

How can Ben get back in touch with
Rory Polestar? Will they ever be virtual
friends again? Find out what happens
to Ben as he puts his helmet and
gloves back on ...

You can order this book directly from Macmillan
Distribution Ltd, Brunel Road, Houndmills, Basingstoke,
Hampshire RG21 6XS   Tel: 01256 302699